Mommy Loves Her Baby

by Tara Jaye Morrow

pictures by Tiphanie Beeke

HarperCollins Publishers

Library of Congress Cataloging-in-Publication Data
Morrow, Tara Jaye.
Mommy loves her baby, Daddy loves his baby / by Tara Jaye Morrow ;
pictures by Tiphanie Beeke.
p.   cm.
Summary: Compares the love Mommy and Daddy have for their baby
to the things that various animals love to do.
ISBN 0-06-029077-3. — ISBN 0-06-029078-1 (lib. bdg.).
[1. Parent and child—Fiction.   2. Love—Fiction.   3. Animals—Fiction.   4. Stories in rhyme.]
I. Beeke, Tiphanie, ill.   II. Title.
PZ8.3.M837 Mo 2003
[E]—dc21   2002068560
CIP
AC

Typography by Stephanie Bart-Horvath
1 2 3 4 5 6 7 8 9 10
❖
First Edition

This book is dedicated to my Mommy, Marlene E. Centeio,
and my Daddy, John F. Centeio, whose love and support
continue to lift me higher.
—T.J.M.

For Anna with Love

—T.B.

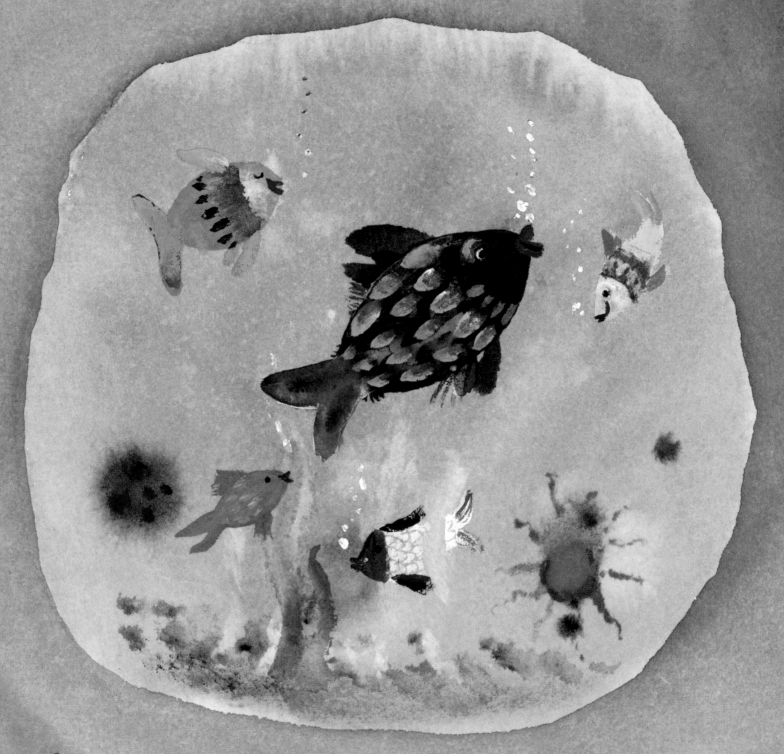

Mommy loves her baby like the fishies love the seas.

like the monkeys love bananas

and the squirrels love the trees.

Mommy loves her baby like the penguins love to slide,

like hyenas love to giggle
and chameleons love to hide.

Mommy loves her baby like the lions love to ROAR.

like the beavers love to paddle
and the eagles love to soar.

Mommy loves her baby like the bear cubs love to rest,

like the horsies love to gallop

and the robins love to nest.

Mommy loves her baby like the owls love to "whooooo,"

like the turkeys love to gobble

and the cows just love to "mooooo!"

moooO

Mommy loves her baby like the froggies love to leap,

like the kitties love to cuddle

and the chickies love to "peep."

Mommy loves her baby, and you know why this is true?
'Cause her baby is the sweetest little,
cutest little
YOU!

FLIP THIS BOOK

FLIP THIS BOOK

Daddy loves his baby, and you know why this is true?
'Cause his baby is the sweetest little, cutest little
YOU!

like the cheetahs love to run and the birdies love to sing.

Daddy loves his
baby like gorillas
love to swing,

and
the bats
just love
to sleep.

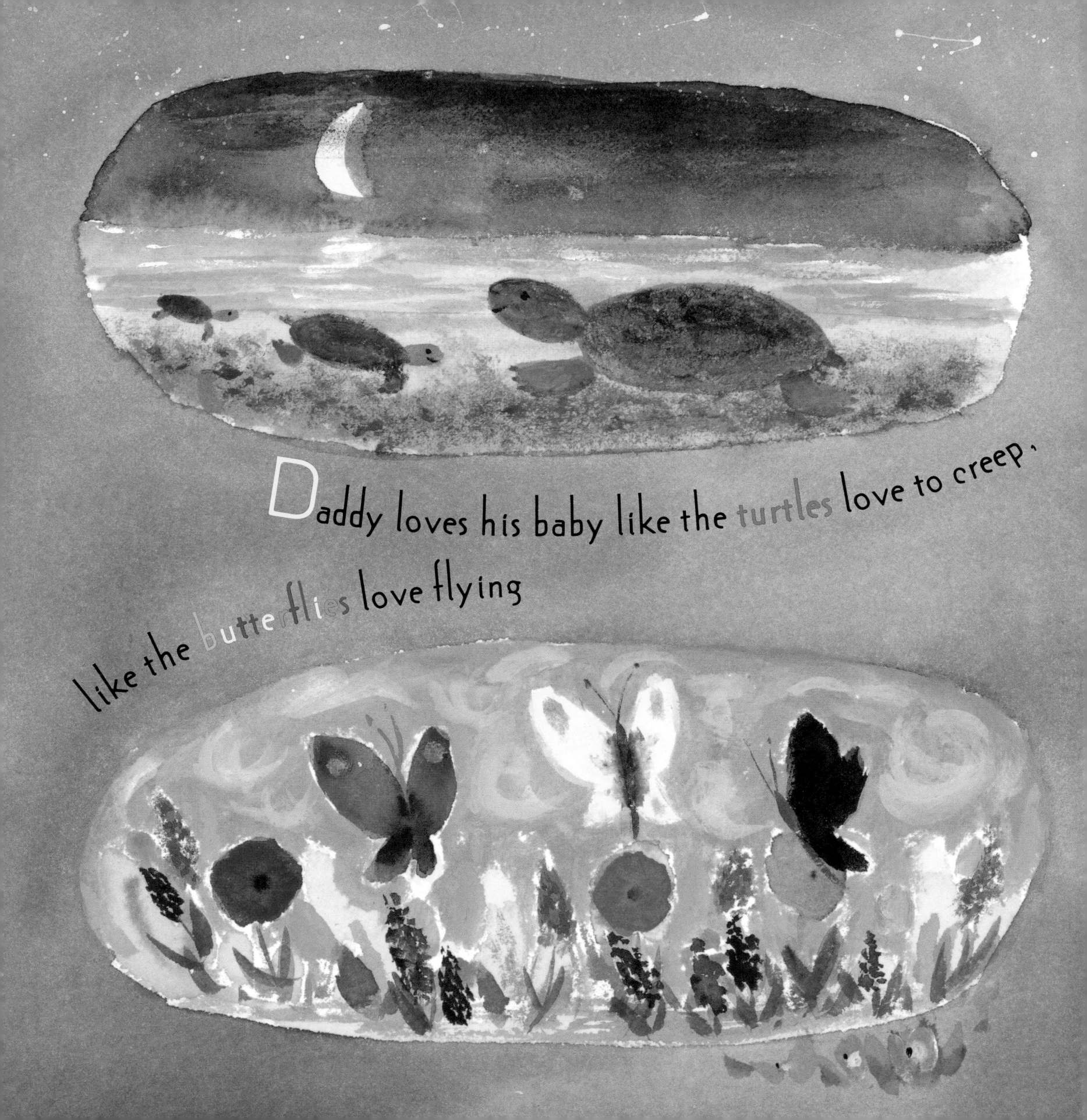

Daddy loves his baby like the turtles love to creep,

like the butterflies love flying

like the roosters love to wake us with a

"rock-a-doodle-doo!"

Daddy loves his baby like the pandas love to chew,

and the llamas love to lick.

Daddy loves his baby like the donkeys love to kick,

like the camels love to carry

like giraffes just love to s-t-r-e-t-c-h

and the gators love to snap.

Daddy loves his baby like the puppies love to yap,

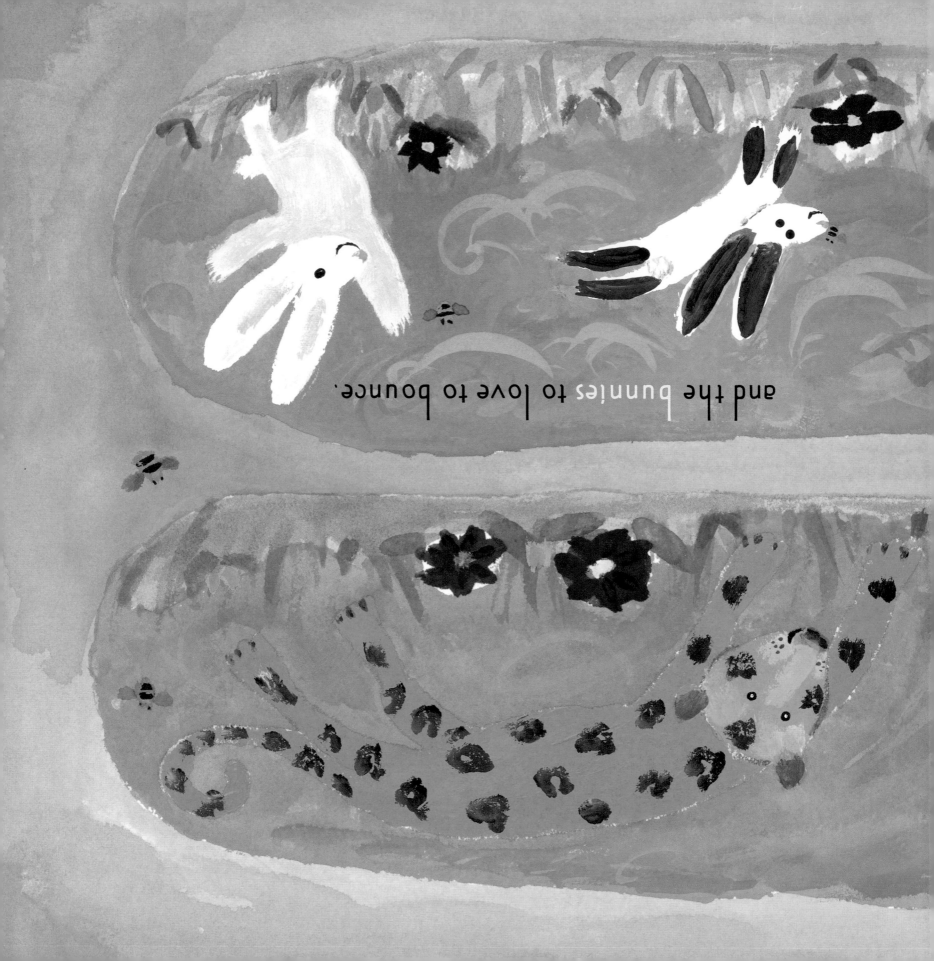

and the bunnies to love to bounce.

like the bumblebees love buzzing

Daddy loves his baby like the leopards love to pounce,

Daddy Loves His Baby

by Tara Jaye Morrow

pictures by Tiphanie Beeke

HarperCollins Publishers

DATE DUE

JAN 2 3 2016